MAID MARIAN AND HER MERRY MEN

GRR!

EEK!

THE WHITISH KNIGHT

Tony Robinson

Illustrated by Paul Cemmick

BBC Books

This book is based on the BBC TV series
Maid Marian and her Merry Men
by Tony Robinson, produced by Richard Callanan
and directed by David Bell.

Published by BBC Books
a division of BBC Enterprises Ltd
Woodlands, 80 Wood Lane, London W12 0TT

First published 1990

ISBN 0 563 36041 0

Printed and bound in Great Britain by Cooper Clegg Ltd, Tewkesbury
Colour separations by Technik Ltd, Berkhamsted
Cover printed by Richard Clay Ltd, St Ives Plc

WELCOME TO ENGLAND IN THE TWELFTH CENTURY! (YOU'RE WELCOME TO IT!)
NOTTINGHAM CASTLE
SHERWOOD FOREST
WORKSOP VILLAGE
EARLY ONE TUESDAY MORNING IN 1195 –
O.K. SNAIL! COME OUT! I'VE GOT YOU SURROUNDED!
GO AWAY!
I WANT MY BREAKFAST AND YOU'RE IT!
OH, PLEASE, GREAT SNAIL GOD IN THE SKY! HEAR MY PLEA!
DISTANT THUNDERING NOISE!
YOU MIGHT AS WELL COME OUT! THERE'S NO ESCAPE!
...PLEASE SEND DOWN DOOM AND DESTRUCTION ON THE HEAD OF THIS HUNGRY HEDGEHOG!
MUCH NEARER THUNDERING NOISE!
WHAT THE..?
THUD!
SQUISH!
WOW! THANK YOU SNAIL GOD!
DON'T MENTION IT!

MYSTERIOUS CELESTIAL SINGING VOICES!
OOOH! THE WHITE KNIGHT!
HE WAS DRESSED IN WHITE-
AND HE WAS A KNIGHT!
WHAT A LOUSY KNIGHT!
THAT'S WHY THEY CALLED HIM-
OOOH! THE WHITE KNIGHT!

OOOH! THE WHITE KNIGHT!

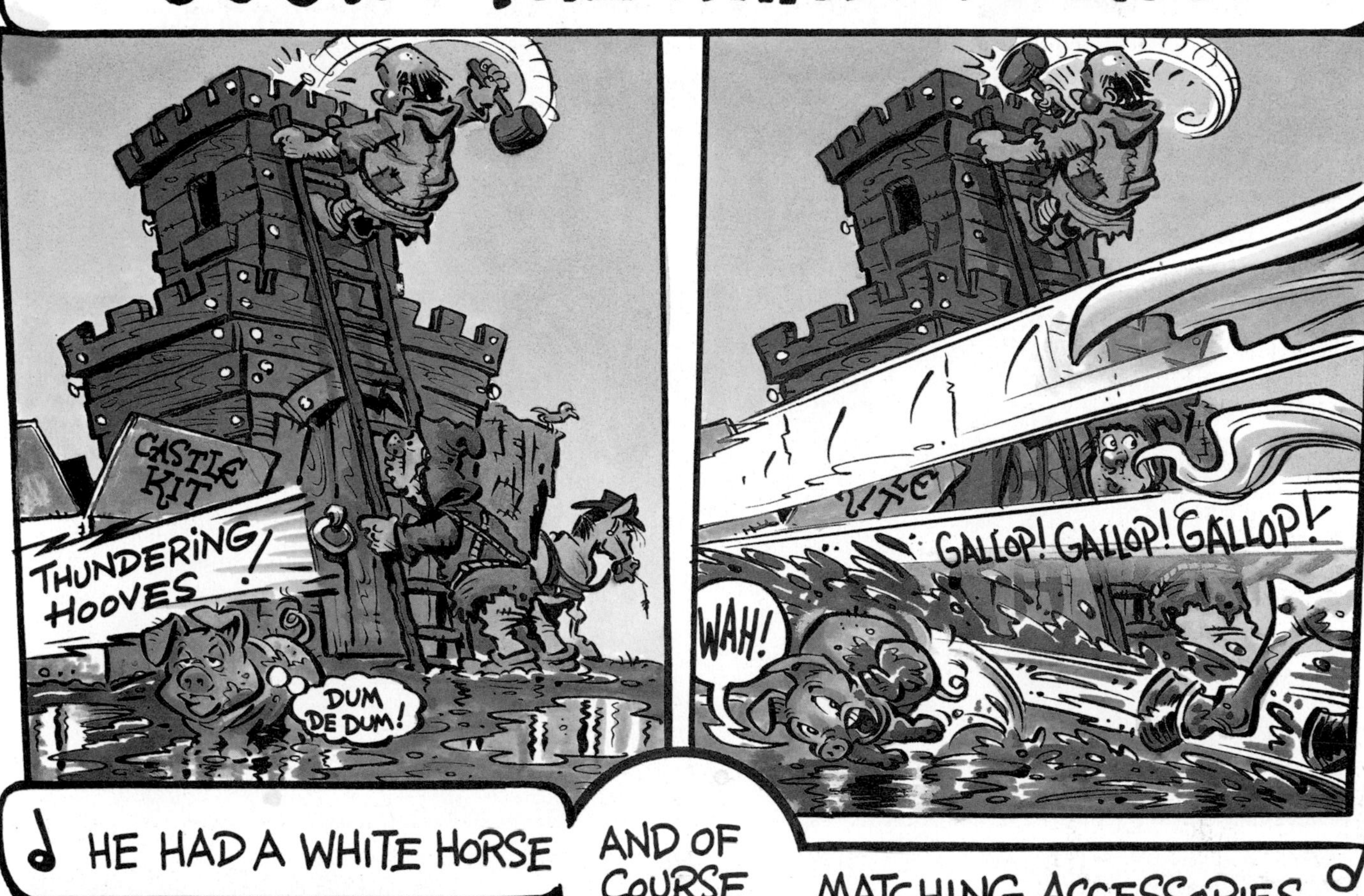

HE HAD A WHITE HORSE

AND OF COURSE

MATCHING ACCESSORIES...

OOOH! THE WHITE KNIGHT!

NESTLING IN A SEA OF MUD ON THE EDGE OF NOTTINGHAM FOREST IS THE VILLAGE OF WORKSOP –
MAID MARIAN IS ADDRESSING THE VILLAGERS –
NOW GATHER ROUND! CONCENTRATE AT THE BACK, PLEASE!
I'VE SOMETHING VERY IMPORTANT TO TELL YOU!
OH, NO! IT'S THAT BOSSY BOOTS, AGAIN!
AS YOU KNOW, WE IN THE MERRY MEN ROB FROM THE RICH AND GIVE TO THE POOR! WELL...
THUNDER!
THUNDER!

SPLATTER!

COME ON, CONCENTRATE! AS YOU KNOW...
DID YOU SEE HIM?
THUNDER
THUNDER!
RUFF!
BLIMEY!
COR!
HECK!
EH?
'STREUTH!
WELL SPLATTER ME!

FLIPPIN' JUGGERNAUTS! YOU SHOULD REPORT HIM!
I WILL! WHAT'S HIS NAME?
OOOH! THE WHITE KNIGHT!
HANG ON! HE'S NOT WHITE! HE'S A SORT OF CREAMY, BEIGEY COLOUR!
YEAH!
THE CREAMY BEIGEY KNIGHT!
YOU CAN'T CALL HIM THE CREAMY BEIGEY KNIGHT! IT'S RIDICULOUS!
WELL YOU CERTAINLY CAN'T CALL HIM THE WHITE KNIGHT! THAT'S A ZONKING GREAT FIB!
WELL, WHAT CAN WE CALL HIM, THEN?
ERR... THE WHITISH KNIGHT?
HMMM, O.K.! NOW CAN WE GET ON, PLEASE?
THE
THE
TOAD
OOOH! THE WHITISH KNIGHT!
SNAIL VOICE CHOIR

MEANWHILE AT NOTTINGHAM CASTLE–
WHERE'S MY BREAKFAST?

CAN YOU STOP SHOUTING! MY KIDS ARE TRYING TO SLEEP!
GET OUT! YOU'VE GONE COLD!
BOOT!
YE MEDIEVAL BED WARMER by appointment to H.M. KING JOHN
WELL I'VE GOT BAD CIRCULATION!
TO YE KITCHENS
COMING, YOUR HIGHNESS!
MORNIN'!
MORNIN'!
MORNIN'!
MORNIN'!

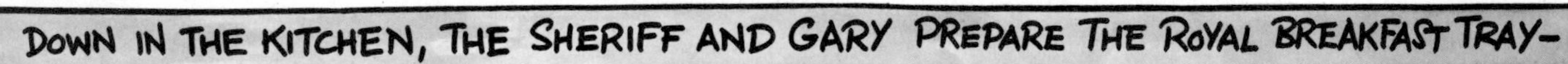
DOWN IN THE KITCHEN, THE SHERIFF AND GARY PREPARE THE ROYAL BREAKFAST TRAY–

MUSHROOMS! TOMATOES! NEWTS! FROGSPAWN! WHAT A REVOLTING MAN HE IS!
THERE'S HIS TEAPOT!
FRESH FROG SPAWN
WAH! I'M TOO YOUNG TO BE BREAKFAST!

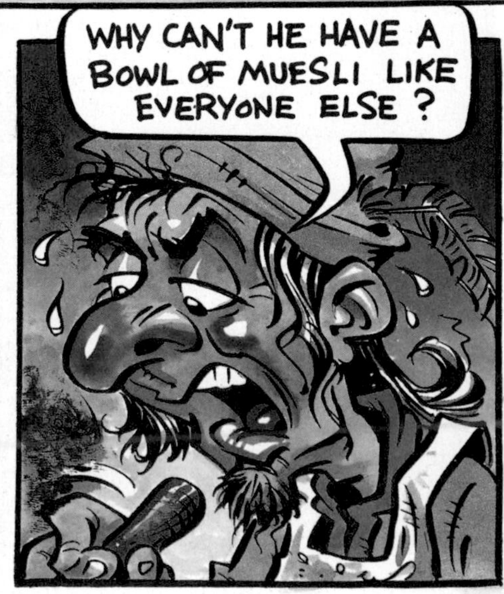
WHY CAN'T HE HAVE A BOWL OF MUESLI LIKE EVERYONE ELSE?

THERE'S HIS TEA-COSY!
NOT THAT IT'LL DO HIM ANY HARM, MORE'S THE PITY! I COULD COVER THE WHOLE LOT IN SULPHURIC ACID AND HE'D STILL SHOVEL IT DOWN AND ASK FOR MORE!
HERE'S HIS PAPER! "'I SWALLOWED A LIVE CHICKEN!' CLAIMS RECORD-BREAKING NUN!" THAT'S INTERESTING ISN'T IT?
YE SPORTS PAGE
NOTTINGHAM FOREST EATEN YET AGAIN
YE DAILY WORKSOP
BATTERING RAM FOUND ON MOON!
NOAH STILL ALIVE SHOCK
AMPUTATION IS GOOD FOR YOU!
WOMAN GIVES BIRTH
NO! IT'S GARBAGE! HE EATS GARBAGE, HE READS GARBAGE AND HE SMELLS LIKE A SUMO WRESTLER'S LAUNDRY BASKET!
FOUL PONG!
TASTE!
BLEURK!
AND HERE'S HIS POST!
OH, DEAR! HIS LIBRARY BOOK'S OVERDUE!
HE'S PROBABLY EATEN IT!
WHAT'S COOKING?
IT'S US!
BIG JOHN
SHOVEL
HOW DO I GET OUT OF THIS BOOK?
DON'T ASK ME, MATE! I'M ONLY AN INCIDENTAL CHARACTER!

ONE BILL, TWO BRIBES, A POSTCARD FROM JERUSALEM AND ONE OF THOSE THINGS ABOUT FRENCH WINDOWS!
JERUSALEM!!!
WHAT'S IT SAY?
"HOW ABOUT INSTALLING THIS ATTRACTIVE PATIO AND FRENCH WINDOWS IN YOUR CASTLE? IT COULD BE CHEAPER THAN YOU THINK!"
YE BEST CUTS of DRAGON
RATATOUILLE
FIRST CATCH YOUR RAT
BOAR BURGERS
NOT THAT! THE POSTCARD!
OH!
"DEAR JOHN, HAVING A WONDERFUL CRUSADE. WISH YOU WERE HERE. BACK ST. SWITHIN'S DAY!"
WHERE'S MY BREAKFAST?
ON MY WAY, YOUR HIGHNESS!
JERUSALEM? THAT'S NOT ENGLAND, IS IT? IT'S FOREIGN! WHO'S IT FROM?
ER..."LOTSA LOVE, DICK!"
GREETINGS FROM THE CRUSADES!
MAYBE I CAN GET OUT THROUGH THE SPINE!

ALL RIGHT ! YES ! YOU TAKE UP HIS BREAKFAST !
NO !

I SAID YOU TAKE UP HIS BREAKFAST !

BUT EVERY TIME I TAKE UP HIS BREAKFAST IT'S BECAUSE YOU KNOW HE'LL BE IN A BAD MOOD! IT'S THAT POSTCARD, ISN'T IT ?
NO, IT ISN'T! NOW I ORDER YOU TO TAKE UP HIS BREAKFAST !
GULP !
NOTTINGHAM ! IF YOU'RE NOT IN FRONT OF ME, PERSONALLY, IN THREE SECONDS FLAT WITH MY BREAKFAST, I'LL DIP YOU IN BUTTER, CUT OFF YOUR CRUSTS AND SERVE YOU UP AS EGGY BREAD !

GRRR !
HERE YOU ARE, YOUR MAJESTY !
POP !
FOUL STINK !
MMM, SMELLS GOOD !
PLOP !
OY !
ABOUT TIME, TOO! WHAT'S IN THE POST ?
OH, THE USUAL !

BACK AT THE VILLAGE-
... AND SO, AT FANTASTIC RISK TO THEMSELVES, MY MERRY MEN HAVE ROBBED THE RICH AND WILL NOW DISTRIBUTE THEIR BOOTY TO YOU- THE POOR !
EAGER ANTICIPATION!
O.K. LITTLE RON ! WHAT HAVE YOU GOT FOR US ?
TA-DAH!
ER...
RUMMAGE!
THIS!
FLOURISH!
TOTAL LACK OF ENTHUSIASM !
ER... YES! WHAT ELSE ?
DON'T ASK!
THIS!
YUK!
UGH!
BLEURK!
WHAT IS IT ?
I THINK IT'S A TABLE DECORATION !

A NAFF HAT AND A TABLE DECORATION! THAT'S WHAT YOU'VE ROBBED FROM THE RICH, IS IT?
HUH! WHAT A REVOLTING PARODY OF MY NOBLE SPECIES!
WELL THERE'S THIS!
AH! ISN'T HE SWEET? HE'S SOOOOOOO SWEEEEEET!
WOT! NO BONES?
LET'S GO FIND YOU A LITTLE FRIEND, SHALL WE?
OH, MUST WE?
WOULD YOU LIKE THIS TEDDY BEAR FOR YOUR VERY OWN?
NO!
OF COURSE YOU WOULD!
NO, I WOULDN'T IT'S REALLY TACKY!
DON'T SAY THAT! YOU'LL MAKE HIM CRY!
WHAT SHALL WE CALL HIM?
RIP OFF!
YES! RIP OFF! THAT'S A NICE NAME!
NO, IT'S NOT!
RIGHT! WHO WANTS THE HAT?
UGH! WHAT A NAFF FLOWER

IN THE KITCHEN AGAIN-
HE IS IN A BAD MOOD, ISN'T HE?
BAD MOOD DOESN'T DESCRIBE IT! HE'S COMPLETELY LOST HIS RAG!
HE CAN HAVE MINE!
IT SUITS HIM!
HE'S ANGRY, GARY! HE'S SCARED AND HIS JOB'S ON THE LINE! WE'RE GOING TO HAVE TO GIVE OUR BELOVED VISITOR THE BIGGEST WELCOME HOME PARTY IN THE HISTORY OF CATERING!
HUH! WOW! I'M STILL ALIVE!
O.K.? OR WE'RE LIKELY TO BE SAWN INTO A THOUSAND PIECES AND SOLD AS A CHRISTMAS JIG-SAW!
MAYBE I SHOULD RE-ENTER THE STORY! BUT I'LL WAIT FOR ANOTHER FOREST SCENE!
YES, SIR! BUT EXCUSE ME, SIR...
I WANT FLAGS AND STREAMERS AND ALL THE OTHER RUBBISH PEOPLE STICK UP WHEN THEY'RE PRETENDING TO HAVE A GOOD TIME!
THANK YOU, NEWT GOD!
YOU'RE WELCOME!
YES, SIR! BUT THERE'S...
I WANT JUGGLERS AND FIRE-EATERS AND A HUGE INFLATABLE PIG'S BLADDER FOR THE KIDS TO JUMP UP AND DOWN ON...
... A BIT OF FOOD...
NOT JUST A BIT OF FOOD, GARY! WE'LL HAVE LOBSTERS IN JELLY, BABY SWANS ON TOAST HEDGEHOGS BAKED IN THEIR JACKETS..
NO! FOOD ON... ON...
HOLD ON! THIS IS THE CREEP WHO FRIED ME!
ON PLATES, GARY! AND BOWLS AND...
YES! I KNOW! THE ROYAL TEA-SET!

NO ONE FRIES SIR ISAAC NEWT AND GETS AWAY WITH IT!
TAKE THIS, PAL!
CHOMP!
YAAARRGHH!
WAH-HA-HA!
NICE ONE, NEWT!
WHAT'S THE ROYAL TEA-SET, SIR?
THROB! ACHE!
YOU KNOW! THAT SWANKY STUFF WILLIAM THE CONQUEROR USED WHEN HE TOOK HIS FAMOUS TEA-BREAK AT THE BATTLE OF HASTINGS!
TEN SIXTY-SIX?
NO! QUARTER PAST ELEVEN, I THINK IT WAS!
WE'LL MAKE THE WHOLE THING A SURPRISE! HE'LL OPEN THE CASTLE GATE, HE'LL HAVE BEEN AWAY FOR YEARS AND THERE'LL BE NO ONE THERE TO MEET HIM AND THEN... AND THEN...
OH, YES! THAT'LL BE REALLY SWEET! HE'LL LOVE THAT!
WHAT?
HOW LONG HAVE WE GOT? WHEN'S HE BACK?
ST. SWITHIN'S DAY!
AND WHEN'S THAT?
WAH!
ERMM...
OH, COME ON! THINK! ST. SWITHIN'S DAY! WHEN ON EARTH IS IT?
HELLO! HAPPY ST. SWITHIN'S DAY!

WORKSOP VILLAGE AGAIN –
SAY! NOT BAD!
NOW LET ME GET THIS CLEAR! MY MEN HAVE SPENT THE ENTIRE MORNING RISKING TORTURE AND DEATH IN ORDER TO PROVIDE YOU WITH HATS, TABLE DECORATIONS AND SOFT TOYS – AND NOT ONE OF YOU WANTS THEM ?!?!
GET OUT AND CHOP SOME WOOD!
HE'S A BIT HEN-PECKED!
ANY MINUTE NOW I'LL MAKE A DRAMATIC ENTRANCE!
NOPE! NOT REALLY!
THIS IS SO HUMILIATING!
HMM, BRUNCH!
IT'S RUBBISH!
EVEN IN 1195 THIS WAS AN OLD JOKE!
ENJOY YOUR TRIP? HA-HA-HA!
TRIP!
NOTHING ELSE WE CAN DO TO HELP YOU, THEN?
EEK!
SWOOP!
SWIPE!
NOPE!

SNORT!
O.K. FINE! THANKS FOR YOUR ATTENTION! COME ON, LADS!
RASP!
WE'RE WASTING OUR TIME! WE'LL GO TO ANOTHER VILLAGE WHERE WE'LL BE APPRECIATED! WHERE PEOPLE REALISE WE'RE A... WE'RE A... WHAT'S THE WORD?
RIP OFF!!!
I BEG YOUR PARDON?
IF THEY DON'T WANT HIM, I DO!
RIP OFF! I'M COMING!
COME ON, ROBIN!
HELP!
SHH!
TO ANOTHER VILLAGE
CREEP!
CREEP!
NOW! THIS IS MY BIG MOMENT!
WHAT A BUNCH OF CREEPS!

O.K. SNAIL! COME OUT! THERE'S NO ESCAPE!
GO AWAY!
RIGHT MEN, THERE'S THE VILLAGE! SEARCH THE HUTS FOR FOOD, THEN ROUND UP THE LITTLE ONES, GIVE THEM A GOING OVER WITH THE NIT COMB AND BRING THEM TO THE CASTLE!
ONLY THE LITTLE ONES, MIND YOU!
OY! ARTIST! THERE'S NOT ENOUGH RABBITS IN THIS STRIP!
THE END OF A BIG MOMENT
YUM!
OH, GREAT SNAIL GOD IN THE SKY, SEND DOWN RETRIBUTION ON THE HEAD OF THIS CROW!
AND REMEMBER! THE PEOPLE OF THIS COMMUNITY LOOK TO US FOR LAW AND ORDER! SO NO VIOLENCE UNLESS IT'S ABSOLUTELY NECESSARY!
SLICE!
WOW! THANKS AGAIN, SNAIL GOD!
NO PROBLEM!
CHARGE!
TUG! TUG!
YEEEHAAARRR!!!
EEK!
AARGH!
OH, NO!
SCREAM!
SHRIEK!
MUM!
OOOH! THE WHITISH KNIGHT!
THE QUAIL VOICE CHOIR

MEANWHILE, IN THE SECRET FOREST HIDE-OUT OF MAID MARIAN'S MERRY BAND, BARRINGTON AND RABIES ARE EXCERCISING THEIR MINDS WITH AN INTELLECTUAL GAME OF—
SNAP!
RIGHT! THAT'S IT! YOU'RE REDUNDANT!
PACK UP YOUR BOWS AND ARROWS AND GET DOWN TO THE DOLE OFFICE!
WHAT DO YOU MEAN?
EIGHT VILLAGES WE'VE BEEN TO- EIGHT! AND DID THE PEASANTS RUSH OUT OF THEIR HOUSES SHOUTING, "HOORAY! IT'S THOSE NICE HELPFUL MERRY MEN!"? NO! THEY JUST MADE RUDE COMMENTS ABOUT OUR TASTE IN TABLE DECORATIONS!
SNIFF!
LET'S FACE IT! NO ONE WANTS OUR HELP! WE'RE ABOUT AS MUCH USE AS A REINDEER AT A CRICKET MATCH!
I'M SORRY LADS! I'M AFRAID WE'RE NOT THE MERRY MEN ANY LONGER! WE'RE THE MISERABLE UNEMPLOYED MEN!
OH, NO! THIS CAN'T BE THE END OF THE BOOK! IT'S ONLY PAGE 17!

NEVER MIND! IT WAS GOOD WHILE IT LASTED! IT WAS BETTER THAN BEING ON A TRAINING SCHEME!
YOU COULD HANG YOUR WOOLLY ON IT!
PARDON?
WHEN IT WAS YOUR TURN TO BOWL YOU COULD TAKE YOUR WOOLLY OFF AND HANG IT ON THE REINDEER'S ANTLERS!
FINDING ANOTHER JOB FOR YOU ISN'T GOING TO BE EASY, IS IT, RABIES?
IF ONLY THE KING WERE HERE!
YES! HE COULD CHOP OFF OUR HEADS AND PUT US OUT OF OUR MISERY!
NO, NOT JOHN! HIS BROTHER, THE REAL KING!
WHAT, RICHARD?
YES! IF HE CAME BACK THINGS WOULD BE DIFFERENT, WOULDN'T THEY?
I DON'T KNOW! HE HASN'T BEEN HERE FOR YEARS! HE'S BEEN OFF ON THE FIRST CRUSADE, SHOOTING ARABS IN BEIRUT!
HE'S NOBLE AND KIND AND LOVES HIS PEOPLE!
YEAH! BEFORE HE LEFT ENGLAND, HE SAID TO KING JOHN, "BROTHER, WHILE I'M AWAY, RULE MY SUBJECTS WISELY AND WELL FOR IF THOU DOST NOT, THEN ON MY RETURN, I SHALL GIVE YOU A RIGHT GOING OVER!"
CHEER UP, YOU LOT! AT LEAST YOU HAVEN'T BEEN FRIED THIS MORNING!
OR STOOD ON!
THEY ALL LOOK AS SICK AS PARROTS!

AND HE'S REALLY GENTLE AND ALL THE FOREST CREATURES LOVE HIM!
ROAST STOAT!
NO, WE DON'T! WE'VE NEVER HEARD OF HIM!
THERE'S STILL NOT ENOUGH RABBITS!
YEAH! AND IF HE WAS AT A CRICKET MATCH, ALL THE REINDEER WOULD COME UP TO HIM AND LICK HIM!
NO, WE WOULDN'T!
I WOULD!
THE VERY ENDANGERED SHURDLEVINKLEFOUT!
AND I BET HE'S REALLY DISHY, TOO! ALL STRONG AND THOUGHTFUL AND DEPENDABLE! THE SORT OF BLOKE YOU'D GO TO IF YOU WERE IN REAL TROUBLE!
LIKE US?
US!
YOU LIVE IN ANOTHER WORLD, DON'T YOU, ROBIN? PEOPLE THINK WE'RE A JOKE!
THAT'S NOT TRUE!
YES, IT IS! PEOPLE WOULD GO TO AN ARMLESS OCTOPUS BEFORE THEY CAME TO US FOR HELP!
HELP!
YUK! WHAT A DISGUSTING IDEA!

MARIAN! WE WANT HELP!!!
IT'S THE SHERIFF AND HIS MEN! THEY'VE STOLEN OUR FOOD AND TAKEN OUR CHILDREN OFF TO THE CASTLE!
YES! AND THEY TOOK MY PET HEDGEHOG AND THEY'RE GOING TO BAKE HIM IN HIS JACKET! AND IT'S A BRAND NEW JACKET!
SOB!
WELL I'M NOT SURE! WE'VE CLOSED THE OFFICE, YOU SEE! THERE ISN'T ANY CALL FOR MERRY MEN ROUND HERE!
RUBBISH! OF COURSE WE'LL HELP YOU!
OH, THANK YOU! THANK YOU! THANK YOU! THANK YOU! etc. etc...
ALL RIGHT! ALL RIGHT! LEAVE ME TO HANDLE THIS, PLEASE!
YES, GOOD PEOPLE OF WORKSOP! WE WILL COME TO YOUR RESCUE! IN THE NAME OF KING RICHARD, THE TRUE MONARCH OF ALL ENGLAND, THE MERRY MEN WILL FREE YOUR CHILDREN FROM THE TYRANT'S GRASP!
TO NOTTINGHAM!
HOORAY!

MEANWHILE AT NOTTINGHAM CASTLE –
WAIL!
BOO-HOO!
HOWL!
I WANT MY MUM!
I WANT HER MUM, TOO!
WHAT LOVELY SINGING!
SHUT UP!
SUDDEN SILENCE!
THANK YOU! NOW, THIS IS YOUR UNCLE GARY! THIS IS YOUR UNCLE GRAEME!
AND I'M YOUR UGLY RAT!
AND I'M YOUR UNCLE SHERIFF!

NOW, WE'VE BROUGHT YOU HERE BECAUSE THIS AFTERNOON WE'VE GOT A VERY SPECIAL GUEST COMING TO THE CASTLE AND YOU'RE GOING TO GIVE HIM A LOVELY SURPRISE!
O.K.?
HEY GUYS! WHAT'S GOING DOWN?
BOO HOO!
SHUT UP!
WHEN HE GETS HERE THERE'LL BE NOBODY ELSE ABOUT! THEN ON THIS TABLE HE'LL SEE A HU-U-U-GE BANQUET AND AT THE VERY MOMENT HE TIPPY-TOES OVER TO IT, YOU'LL BURST OUT OF YOUR HIDEY-HOLES DRESSED IN SWEET LITTLE COSTUMES AND RECITE THIS!
...AND IT'LL BE LOVELY AND PRETTY AND IT'LL MAKE OUR SPECIAL GUEST FEEL ALL WARM INSIDE, WON'T IT? BECAUSE IF HE DOESN'T FEEL ALL WARM INSIDE HE'LL SACK MY BOSS! AND IF HE SACKS MY BOSS, MY BOSS'LL SACK ME AND IF MY BOSS SACKS ME I'LL GET ALL CROSS AND GRUMPY!
AND WHEN I'M CROSS AND GRUMPY IT'S BIG TROUBLE FOR LITTLE CHILDREN!
NICE GUY, HUH?
BOO-HOO!

HOWL! SCREAM! WAIL!
I THINK THEY'RE A BIT SCARED OF YOU, SIR!
NONSENSE! THEY LOVE ME! WATCH THIS!
YEAH! LIKE A COW LOVES A BUTCHER!
HELLO! LITTLE BOY!
GRRR!
GRRR!
LIKE A FLY LOVES A ROLLED-UP NEWSPAPER!
SEE!
THEY ADORE ME! THIS IS GOING TO BE GREAT! I'LL BE KNIGHTED FOR THIS! I'LL BE MADE LORD SHERIFF OF NOTTINGHAM FOREST!
AH, WE HATE NOTTINGHAM FOREST!
WE HATE LIVERPOOL, TOO!
YOU GET THEM INTO THEIR COSTUMES AND START REHEARSING!
YOU! COME WITH ME!
WHAT A NICE LITTLE BOY, ISN'T HE?
PAT! PAT!
SOB!
SNIFFLE!
BYE, NOW!
KISS!
THAT MAN IS PATHETIC!

... SO WE JUST KNOCK AT THE CASTLE DOOR, DO WE, AND SAY, "EXCUSE ME, WE'VE COME TO RESCUE THE CHILDREN."?
STOP WHINING, ROBIN! WE'LL THINK OF SOMETHING!
WAIT A MINUTE! THAT CART GIVES ME AN IDEA!
QUICK! IN YOU GET!
BUT WE WON'T BE ABLE TO START IT!
WHY NOT, MAN?
WE HAVEN'T GOT A KEY!
RABIES! YOU DON'T NEED A KEY TO START A HORSE AND CART!
DON'T YOU?
HEY! COME ON, ARTIST! HERE WE ARE IN AN OPEN FIELD AND STILL NO RABBITS!
NO! WE CAN JUMP START IT! LET ME DEMONSTRATE!

YOU TAKE TWO BITS OF WIRE AND STICK THEM IN THE HORSE'S BUM!
BLIMEY, I'M BORED! WHY DOESN'T SOMETHING UNEXPECTED HAPPEN?
LIKE THIS!
JAB!
JAB!
THE HORSE JUMPS AND...
YAAARRGHH!
LET'S GOOOOO!
OY!
HEY YOU! COME BACK WITH OUR CART!
OOOH! THE WHITISH KNIGHT!
THE MOLE VOICE CHOIR!

BACK IN KING JOHN'S BEDROOM-
GLOOM!
ER... SORRY TO BOTHER YOU, YOUR GLORIOUS MAJESTY!
BLOOMIN' CHICKENS!
MRS.'R'- THE CLEANING RODENT
AAARGHH! HE'S HERE, ISN'T HE? I'M RUINED! RUINED!
NO, YOUR MAJESTY! IT'S JUST THAT WE WERE WONDERING IF WE COULD BORROW THE ROYAL TEA-SET!
HIDE!
HIDE!
WHAT?
WELL YOU DO WANT TO MAKE A GOOD IMPRESSION, DON'T YOU?
YES! YES! OF COURSE!

ALL RIGHT! IT'S UNDER THE BED!
SQUAWK!
HEY, BUD! CAN'T A GUY GET A BATH IN PEACE?
BUT IF YOU DAMAGE IT, YOU DIE! IT'S WORTH MORE THAN YOU'VE EARNED IN YOUR ENTIRE LIFE!

WHAT? MORE THAN 85p?
WHAT A CHEEK!
SLIDE!
DO YOU KNOW HOW THIS STUFF CAME INTO MY FAMILY, SLIMEBALL?
NO!

IT WAS GIVEN TO MY GREAT-GREAT-GREAT-GREAT-GREAT-GRANDFATHER, KING WILLIAM WHEN HE SAVED THE LIFE OF THE GRATEFUL MERCHANT!
SO IT'S PRECIOUS TO ME! UNDERSTAND?
ER... YES, SIRE!

IN THE CASTLE COURTYARD-
I KNOW I SHOULDN'T SAY THIS 'COS I MADE THEM MYSELF, BUT I THINK THOSE COSTUMES LOOK REALLY EFFECTIVE!
OH, COME ON! THESE LOOK NOTHING LIKE REAL RABBITS!
NO! AND NEITHER DO YOU!
NOW! HANDS OUT FOR ONE OF THESE!
AND YOU'RE THE CUTEST SO YOU GET THE BIG STICK!
NO ACCOUNTING FOR TASTE, EH?
NOW LET'S DO IT AGAIN WITH THE WORDS AND THE STEPS! BUT THIS TIME TWIDDLE YOUR LITTLE THINGS, O.K.?
ONE-TWO-THREE-FOUR! ONE-TWO-THREE-FOUR! GOD-SAVE-OUR-GREY-SHUS-KING...
POUND! POUND!
EEK!
OH, COME ON! WE'RE REHEARSING! WHOEVER'S THAT?

THAT WAS VERY INTERESTING ABOUT WILLIAM THE CONQUEROR, SIR! HOW DID HE SAVE THE GRATEFUL MERCHANT'S LIFE, THEN?
HE SAID, "IF YOU GIVE ME THAT TEA-SERVICE, I WON'T KILL YOU!
WOW! WHAT A MAGNIFICENT TEA-SET!
GREAT TEA-SETS OF THE WORLD
TO YE COURTYARD
AH! WHAT A LOVELY STORY! IT GIVES YOU A WARM GLOW INSIDE, DOESN'T IT?
YES! LIKE THE FEELING YOU GET WHEN YOU SIT ON A RED-HOT POKER!
YE COURTYARD
RATTLE!
RATTLE!
PIZZA CART
PIZZA CART
PIZZAS?

YES, ME OLD MATEY, 'ERE'S THE ORDER ! FIVE JUMBO-SIZED PIZZAS FOR THE CASTLE !
BUT WE HAVEN'T ORDERED ANY PIZZAS !
ARE WE THERE YET ?
SHUT UP !
EH ?
SHUT UP... ER... SHUT UP SHOP FOR THE NIGHT, I 'AD, WHEN THE ORDER CAME IN ! BUT PIZZAS IS MY TRADE AND WOT I SEZ IS...
OOOH! WHO'S ORDERED PIZZAS ?

I DUNNO WHO ORDERED THEM, SQUIRE! WHAT I SEZ IS IF THE CUSTOMER ORDERS A PIZZA, THE CUSTOMER GETS A PIZZA!
PSSST! THIS WAY, KIDS!
"FIVE JUMBO-SIZED PIZZAS WITH EXTRA OLIVES!"
JONES? JONES? NO ONE OF THAT NAME HERE! LET ME SEE THAT ORDER!
YEAH! IN THE NAME OF JONES!
WAIT A MINUTE! ARE YOU SURE IT'S 'JONES'? IT'S NOT JOHN, IS IT? WE'VE GOT A KING JOHN! NO, HE WOULDN'T HAVE EXTRA OLIVES! HE'D HAVE EXTRA RAT, NEWT AND DEAD GERBIL!
PIZZA CART

SORRY! YOU'LL HAVE TO TAKE YOUR PIZZAS ELSEWHERE! I CAN'T WASTE ANY MORE TIME! I'VE GOT A REHEARSAL TO ATTEND WITH THESE CHIL...
CART
RUMBLE!
GONE!
HANG ON! WHERE'VE THEY GONE?
THEY WERE HERE A MINUTE AGO!
HYAAARRR! GIDDY-UP!
YES, NOW LET'S THINK THIS THROUGH CAREFULLY! WE CAME OUT OF KING JOHN'S BEDROOM...
AND YOU SAID IF YOU'D HAD TO STAY IN THERE ANOTHER MINUTE, YOU'D HAVE THROWN UP ALL OVER HIS BEDSPREAD!
ALL RIGHT! ALL RIGHT! THEN WE WALKED DOWN THE CORRIDOR WITH THE TEA-SET...
THE TEA-SET! WHERE'S THE TEA-SET?
DUMB CLUCKS!

BYE!
HEY, YOU! COME BACK THIS INSTANT!
YOU CAN'T HAVE THAT TEA-SET! IT'S WORTH A FORTUNE!
IS IT? OH, GOOD!
RATTLE!
UGH!
THUD!
HOORAY!!!
ARE YOU ALL RIGHT, SIR?
WHAT'S GOING ON?
WHERE'S MY TEA-SET?

WHICH TEA-SET IS THAT AGAIN, YOUR WONDERFULNESS ?
NOTTINGHAM! HAVE YOU GOT A SORE THROAT ?
NO!
WOULD YOU LIKE ONE ?
NO, MY LORD! CERTAINLY NOT !
GARY! ROUND UP A POSSE !
A THOUSAND GOLD PIECES TO THE MAN WHO FINDS THE TEA-SET !
WILL THIS ONE DO, SIR ?
HISS! SPIT! HISS!
A POSSE, GARY! A POSSE!
YOWL! SCRATCH! SPIT!
NOTTINGHAM !
DON'T WORRY, MY LORD! THEY'LL BE ON THEIR KNEES BEGGING FOR MERCY IN FIVE MINUTES !

LATER, DEEP IN THE DEPTHS OF NOTTINGHAM FOREST—
SNIGGER! GIGGLE!
IN HOW LONG?
GOSH! A ROYAL VISIT!
WOW!
WELL... FIVE MINUTES-ISH!
NO, YOUR WONDERFULNESS! WAIT, PLEASE! DON'T YOU REMEMBER?
NOTTINGHAM, WE'VE BEEN WALKING ROUND IN CIRCLES FOR THREE HOURS! IF WE'VE LOST THEM I'LL TAKE THE TIP OF YOUR TONGUE IN ONE HAND AND WITH THE OTHER I'LL...
OOH! ISN'T HE ROUGH!
WHAT?
TUG!
WELL, IF MY MEMORY SERVES ME CORRECTLY... GRAEME, WOULD YOU GO OVER TO THAT BUSH AND PULL THAT BIG BRANCH, PLEASE?
WHAT? THIS ONE?
POW!

NYAH-HA-HA-HA!
JUST AS I THOUGHT, SIRE! THEIR HIDEOUT SHOULD BE JUST AROUND THE NEXT BUSH!
DROOP!
WOW! WHAT A WONDERFUL TEA-SET!
YEAH! NICE!
EXPERTS ON SHINY OBJECTS!
SEE?
OOH, YES!
PLEASE GO AWAY!
WARNING! OUTLAWS!
SECRET HIDEOUT AHEAD!
KEEP OUT! THIS MEANS YOU!
AND ESPECIALLY YOU TWO!
DANGER! BOOBY TRAPS!
SIRE, MAY I ADD A NOTE OF CAUTION TO THE PROCEEDINGS!
NO, YOU MAY NOT! GET THE TEA-SET AND LET'S GET OUT OF HERE!

IT'S JUST THAT I'VE BEEN IN THIS KIND OF SITUATION BEFORE...
LOOK! DICK'S GOING TO TURN UP AT THE CASTLE ANY MINUTE NOW...
...AND THIS IS EXACTLY THE SORT OF THING WHEN YOU THINK EVERYTHING'S GOING JUST THE WAY YOU WANT IT...
...AND THERE'S NO ONE TO MEET HIM, NO TEA-SET, NO BANQUET, POSSIBLY THE END OF MY HIGHLY PROMISING CAREER - AND CERTAINLY THE END OF YOUR HIGHLY PATHETIC LIFE!
...AND THEN YOU FIND...
NOTTINGHAM!
...THAT YOU'VE BEEN...
KERSPLOOSH!
...LURED INTO...
...A...
...TRAP!
TRIP WIRE
TRIP!
GUESS WHAT THIS IS!

AND DON'T COME ANY CLOSER, PLEASE!
YOU!
AND I WOULD ADVISE YOUR MEN NOT TO DRAW THEIR SWORDS! YOU'RE SURROUNDED NOT ONLY BY A FANATICAL BAND OF WOODLAND TERRORISTS...
...BUT ALSO BY A HIGHLY MILITANT PARISH COUNCIL!
GRRR!
NOT TO MENTION A HERD OF KILLER RABBITS!

YOU ARE, OF COURSE, MOST WELCOME TO HAVE YOUR TEA-SET BACK! BUT FIRST THERE IS THE SMALL MATTER OF THE MONEY!
GLEAM!
GLISTEN!
WHAT MONEY?
THE THOUSAND GOLD PIECES THE SHERIFF OFFERED TO THE MAN WHO FOUND THE TEA-SET!
BUT HE HASN'T GOT A THOUSAND GOLD PIECES! IF HE HAD, HE WOULDN'T BE WORKING FOR ME, WOULD HE? GUARDS! SEIZE IT!
BEFORE YOU DO ANYTHING HASTY, MAY I JUST POINT OUT THAT TIED TO EACH LEG OF THIS WONKY TABLE IS A STRING, THE OTHER END OF WHICH IS ATTACHED TO A SMALL CHILD!
IF YOU TAKE ONE STEP FORWARD, I SHALL GIVE THE ORDER TO PULL AND THE TABLE WILL COLLAPSE!
YEAH! SO THERE!
THAT TEA-SET BELONGS TO THE NATIONAL TRUST! YOU WOULDN'T DARE!
PULL!

TILT!
CRACK!
YANK!
QUICK! SAVE IT SOMEONE!
LEAP!
GRAB!
SLIDE!
I'VE GOT IT, SIRE!
THOUSANDS OF JAPANESE TOURISTS COME TO ENGLAND EVERY YEAR JUST TO SEE IT!
PULL!
TUG!
SNAP!
TILT!
SLIDE!
I'LL SAVE IT, SIRE!
SQUIDGE!
LEAP!
AND ANYWAY, IT'S A THOUSAND GOLD PIECES FOR ANY MAN WHO FINDS IT AND YOU'RE A GIRL!
SHERIFF, THAT'S REALLY SEXIST! LAST TWO LEGS TOGETHER - PULL!
NO!

TUG!
CRACK!
CRACK!
TUG!
OH, WELL SAVED, SIR!
DASH!
GRAB!
TWIRL!
1000 GOLD PIECES
ALL RIGHT! HERE'S YOUR THOUSAND GOLD PIECES! JUST GIVE ME BACK MY TEA-SET! I KNOW WHEN I'M BEATEN!
WAIT!
GASP! IT'S THE WHITISH KNIGHT!
THE MALE MOUSE CHOIR
♫ OOOH, THE WHITISH KNIGHT! ♪

YES! I AM THE WHITISH KNIGHT! BUT NOW I WILL REVEAL MY TRUE IDENTITY!
OH, NO! I RECOGNISE THAT VOICE! IT'S BROTHER DICK!
AND I'M THE WHITISH HORSE!
KING RICHARD!
ALL KNEEL!
KING RICHARD!
KNEELING ALREADY!
KING RICHARD!
SLIDE!
KNEEL
HEE! HEE!
SORRY!

KING RICHARD REMOVES HIS HELMET!
OH, ISN'T HE GORGEOUS? ISN'T HE HUNKY? NOW THAT HE'S HOME AGAIN EVERYTHING'S GOING TO BE ALL RIGHT, ISN'T IT?
ARE YOU BLIND? LOOK AT HIM! HE'S A DEAD RINGER FOR HIS BROTHER! THEY'RE ALL THE SAME THESE ROYALS!
DON'T BE RIDICULOUS!
YOUR HIGHNESS! I AM ONLY A POOR, RATHER ATTRACTIVE, SERVANT GIRL, BUT I BEG YOU GIVE ME LEAVE TO SPEAK!
YOUR REQUEST IS GRANTED!
HAVE YOU SEEN THE POVERTY IN WHICH THESE PEOPLE LIVE!
I HAVE!
AND THE INJUSTICE AND CRUELTY METED OUT TO THEM?
I HAVE!
AND THEIR HOUSES BURNING, THEIR CHILDREN TERRORISED AND THEIR HEDGEHOGS BAKED IN THEIR JACKETS!
INDEED I HAVE AND ALL I CAN SAY IS ...
GOOD POINT!
...WELL DONE!

SORRY?
HEDGEHOGS! I HATE THEM!
JOHN! I THOUGHT YOU'D MAKE A BAD KING! BUT I WAS MISTAKEN! YOU HAVE RULED MY PEOPLE WISELY AND WELL! YOU'VE MAINTAINED LAW AND ORDER, SET UP AN EFFICIENT TAX SYSTEM AND WEEDED OUT THE TROUBLEMAKERS!
WAH!
STOMP!
I DID MY BEST!
I CAN GO BACK TO BEIRUT NOW WITH MY MIND AT REST, KNOWING THAT YOU AND YOUR MEN ARE MAKING ENGLAND GREAT AGAIN!
HOO RAY!
HOO-RAY!!!
HOO-RAY!!!
GOD SAVE OUR GRACIOUS KING! LISTEN WHILE WE DO OUR THING! LOTS OF RULERS AREN'T MUCH COP - BUT TO US YOU ARE THE TOP! THOUGH YOU TRAVEL FAR AWAY - KILLING PEOPLE NIGHT AND DAY! AS ACROSS THE DUNES YOU ROAM, DON'T FORGET YOUR FRIENDS BACK HOME!
RICHARD I
RICHARD THE FIRST! YEAH!
GOD BLESS YOU, YOUR ROYAL HIGHNESS!
THANK YOU! I'M SURE HE WILL!

OH, ONE SMALL THING, JOHNNIE!
HERO PERSON AND BEAR MAN
WE AREN'T IN THIS STORY!
YES, DICKY?
THE LITTLE CREEP WHO DID THE DEMOLITION JOB ON OUR CROCKERY!
MMNNN?
HOW SHALL WE PUNISH HIM?
MAKE HIM EAT EVERY LAST BIT OF IT?
YES! THEN WASH IT DOWN WITH A GALLON OF QUICK-DRY GLUE!
MMNNN! AND SHAKE HIM UP AND DOWN UNTIL IT'S ALL STUCK BACK TOGETHER AGAIN!
AND SQUEEZE HIM SO HARD THE ENTIRE TEA SERVICE COMES OUT AGAIN CUP BY CUP!
OH, NOTTINGHAM!
YES, YOUR ROYAL HIGHNESSES?
CREEP!
COME ON!
TEA TIME!
SNIGGER! GIGGLE!
TO NOTTINGHAM
OH, OH! THANK YOU! THANK YOU!

SO THAT'S IT, IS IT? BACK TO THE VILLAGE FLOGGING DEAD RATS!
AND BASHING MY HEAD AGAINST TREES!
AND BEING AN IDIOT!
AND MAKING SWANKY UNDERWEAR FOR NOBLEMEN!
WHAT?
DO YOU WANT TO SPEND THE REST OF YOUR DAYS SITTING BY THE FIRE IN COMFORT AND SAFETY?
WELL...
COME OUT, SNAIL! I WANT MY DINNER!
OH, NO! NOT AGAIN! O.K. SNAIL GOD! DO YOUR STUFF!
OR WOULD YOU RATHER LIVE A LIFE OF DANGER, HARDSHIP AND ADVENTURES?
WE MAY BE JUST A SMALL BAND BUT OUR NAME WILL BLAZE THROUGH HISTORY LIKE A ... LIKE A... BIG BLAZER! WE'LL BE LEGENDS FOR EVER AND EVER AND IN YEARS TO COME, PEOPLE WILL WATCH OUR STORY ON LITTLE GLOWING BOXES, WON'T THEY?
DISTANT THUDDING NOISE!
YUM! YUM! DROOL!
AH! HERE HE COMES TO SAVE ME, NOW!
I'M GLAD YOU ASKED ME THAT, BECAUSE...
YEAH!!!
MUCH NEARER THUDDING NOISE!
WHAT THE...?
WOW! HE'S COME IN PERSON THIS TIME!
MAID MARIAN AND HER MERRY MEN WILL NEVER DIE, WILL THEY ROBIN?
WAH!
SQUELSH!
HOO-RAY!
ISN'T THERE ANYTHING ELSE ON, DEAR?
I SUPPOSE NOT! ALL RIGHT! BACK TO THE FOREST IT IS THEN! PEOPLE WATCHING US ON GLOWING BOXES! HONESTLY!
OH, THANKS A LOT, PAL!
YES! IT'S MOLUSC MAN OUT FOR A JOG!
DON'T MENTION IT!
YE END!
Paul Cemmick (with thanks to colourful Nadia)